Open Anywhere

SHORT STORY WRITING PROMPTS

First published in Australia in 2025 by BookTree Publishing.

Copyright © 2026 by Katy More

All rights reserved.

No part of this publication may be reproduced, stored, transmitted, or distributed in any form or by any means, electronic or otherwise, without prior written permission from the publisher, except for brief quotations in reviews or educational discussion.

This pubwlication was created using a combination of human authorship and AI-assisted drafting. All content has been curated, edited, and shaped by the author.

ISBN: 978-1-7640196-5-1
Cover Designed: Adobe FireFly

Produced by Scribbly.com.au
Printed and bound in Australia by

PO Box 105
Narangba Qld 4504
Australia

www.booktreepublishing.com.au

A Note from the Author

Short stories have always felt like small rooms with open doors.

You can step into them quickly. You can leave them when you need to. You can explore a single moment without committing to a long journey before you are ready. For many writers, short stories are where confidence is born. They are where voice begins to sound like itself.

I created this collection after years of sitting beside writers — in libraries, workshops, quiet conversations, and online spaces — listening to the same question arise again and again: *Where do I begin?*

The world is now full of writing prompts, tools, and technologies offering instant ideas. That abundance can be inspiring. It can also be overwhelming.

In developing this book, I made thoughtful use of modern tools — including AI-assisted drafting — to generate a wide field of possibilities. But this collection is not an automated list. It is a curated companion, built with care, tested with writers, and guided by lived experience in writing communities.

This book is not asking you to produce perfect stories. It is offering you doorways into moments — beginnings, turning points, quiet endings — that you may enter at your own pace. Some will call to you immediately. Others will wait. Trust that instinct. It is part of your voice forming itself.

If you write one complete short story, that is

wonderful. If you write fragments, sketches, or single scenes, that is equally valuable. Every sentence is a step deeper into the craft.

I hope these pages become a familiar place to return to. Remember:

> *Stories can be small and still meaningful.*
>
> *Beginnings can be simple.*
>
> *Writing can be gentle.*

Wherever your stories lead, I'm grateful you've invited this book into your journey.

Warmly,

*For the writers of short stories —
those who came before,
those writing now,
and those still gathering the courage to begin.*

Notes:

How to Use This Collection

This collection was created for one simple reason: to help you write — not someday, not when life is quieter, but right now, with the time and energy you have.

Each book in this series follows the same pattern. Once you've used one volume, you'll know exactly how to use the next. No complicated rules. No theory-heavy lectures. Just open, choose a prompt, and begin.

Inside, you'll find clusters of prompts to spark ideas, creative boosters to shake things loose when you're stuck, and writing challenges to stretch you a little further when you're ready. Some days you might write for five minutes. Other days you'll disappear into a scene and look up hours later, surprised by what came out. Both count.

There's no correct order. No gold star for finishing every page. Some prompts will speak to you immediately. Others will wait patiently until you need them. Trust that.

Write messily. Write quickly. Write badly if you must. The magic isn't in getting it right the first time — it's in showing up at the page and letting the words find you.

So open anywhere.
Your next story is already waiting.

Quick Start Guide

There are no lengthy instructions waiting for you here, and no rules to follow. Only a gentle invitation to begin. Unsure how? Here is a suggestion to help you find your first step.

Step One — Open Anywhere: You can read in front-to-back order or let the book fall open where it wants to. Trust the page or prompt that finds you.

Step Two — Choose a Prompt: Read the cluster introduction. Skim the prompts. Notice which one gives you a tiny flicker of curiosity. That's your prompt.

Step Three — Set a Timer: Five minutes if you're busy. Twenty if you have the space. A full hour if you're disappearing into your story. Any time counts.

Step Four — Write Without Editing: Don't fix spelling. Don't reword sentences. Don't backspace. Let the words arrive however they arrive.

Step Five — Stop When the Timer Ends: Underline the sentence/s you like. Circle the idea/s you might return to. Close the book feeling proud that you showed up.

Other Ways to Use This Book

- Dip into the Creative Boosters when you're stuck
- Roll the Prompt Dice when you want surprise combinations
- Try the Writing Challenges when you feel ready to stretch Use prompts in writing groups or classrooms
- Return to favourite pages again and again

Always Remember:

Some days writing will feel easy. Other days it won't. Both are normal. The only real success is putting words on the page.

Open anywhere.

Start small.

Keep going.

Your stories are closer than you think.

A Note on Timers

Several of the challenges in this book suggest writing for a set period of time. For some writers, the word timer immediately conjures an image of a loud alarm, a ticking stopwatch, or pressure to race against the clock. That is not the intention here.

A timer is simply a boundary. A small agreement with yourself: for this length of time, I will stay with the page. Nothing more.

Your timer can be anything that marks passing time gently. A kitchen timer with the sound turned off. A clock on the wall. A playlist of three songs. The length of a cup of tea cooling beside you. Until the washing machine has finished.

Some writers prefer no device at all. They simply write until they feel a natural pause, then check the time afterward. This is equally valid.

The purpose of timed writing is not speed. It is permission. When the end point is known, the mind relaxes into the task. The inner critic quiets. Words arrive more freely.

Choose whatever method feels kind.

The page does not need urgency.

It only needs your presence.

Contents

How to Use This Collection | 09

Quick Start Guide | 10

A Note on Timers | 12

PART ONE: WARM-UP & MINDSET | 15

Why Short Stories Matter | 17

Using This Collection | 18

Preparing Your Writing Space | 18

Five-Minute Warm-Up Prompts | 19

PART TWO: CORE PROMPT COLLECTION | 21

Cluster 1 — The Unexpected Beginning | 25

Cluster 2 — A Moment That Changes Everything | 28

Cluster 3 — Secrets and Revelations | 31

Cluster 4 — The Stranger | 34

Cluster 5 — The Ordinary Made Strange | 37

Cluster 6 — The Choice | 40

Cluster 7 — The Disruption | 43

Cluster 8 — The Quiet Ending | 46

PART THREE: CREATIVE BOOSTERS | 49

Twist Generators | 51

Character Sparks | 52

Setting Sparks | 53

Object Prompts | 54

Dialogue Starters | 54

First-Line Hooks | 55

PART FOUR: ADVANCED WRITING CHALLENGES | 57

The 30-Minute Story Sprint | 59

Writing Under Constraint | 60

Perspective Shifts | 61

Genre-Bending Stories | 61

Story-in-a-Day Challenge | 62

PART FIVE: BONUS WRITER TOOLS| 63

Prompt Dice Tables | 65

Random Prompt Picker | 67

Monthly Writing Tracker | 67

SAMPLE: MONTHLY WRITING TRACKER | 69
NOTE PAGES | 73

About the *Open Anywhere* Series | 82

About the Author | 84

About the Publisher | 85

Part One

WARM-UP & MINDSET

Notes:

Warm-Up & Mindset

Before beginning, it helps to pause for a moment remember that writing does not require perfect conditions or elaborate preparation. It asks only for attention — a willingness to meet the blank space and see what might emerge.

This opening section is designed to settle you into that space. Nothing here is compulsory. You can skip this section if you wish. There are no rules to master before you proceed. This is simply a gentle threshold between intention and action.

Why Short Stories Matter

Short stories occupy a unique place in a writer's practice. They are compact enough to complete, yet expansive enough to carry meaning. Within a few pages, you learn to choose a moment worth exploring, to shape tension, to listen for voice, and to discover how endings echo.

For new writers, short stories offer manageable beginnings. For returning writers, they provide a way back to rhythm. For experienced writers, they remain laboratories — places to experiment with form, tone, and perspective without the long arc of a novel pressing overhead.

It is not uncommon for writers find their voice in a single short piece written almost by accident. Many larger works began as scenes first discovered in brief form. Each story you write strengthens instinct and confidence, regardless of whether it is ever shared.

Perfection is not the objective here. Presence is.

Using This Collection

This book is intended as a working companion. It is not a course and not a curriculum. There is no prescribed order and no expectation that every prompt will be completed.

Each cluster contains a short introduction, a set of core prompts, optional expansions, and a challenge for those moments when you wish to stretch further. Later sections provide creative boosters and structured writing exercises to draw upon when momentum slows or curiosity calls.

You may choose to move through clusters sequentially. Or you may open the book at random. All approaches are equally valid. It can be a good idea to mark the pages you enjoy so you can return repeatedly to favourite prompts.

The only requirement is that you respond to what interests you.

Preparing Your Writing Space

Writing happens in many places. At a desk. At a kitchen table. In a notebook balanced on a knee. On a phone screen before sleep. There is no single correct environment.

Choose a space that allows you to linger without self-consciousness. Gather whatever tools feel natural — pen, keyboard, timer, or none at all. The aim is not to create ceremony, but permission.

When you sit down to write, you mark a small boundary in your day. On one side is everything else. On the other is this page.

That boundary is the perfect beginning.

Five-Minute Warm-Up Prompts

When the mind feels crowded or hesitant, brief warm-ups help loosen the first words. Here is a quick warm-up exercise for you should you need it.

Pick one prompt from the below list, set a timer for five minutes and write continuously. Do not edit or correct. Allow the sentences to arrive as they will. Five minutes is enough to open the door.

1. Describe the last room you entered.
2. Begin with the sentence: I didn't expect that day to end this way…
3. List five sounds around you, then build a scene from one of them.
4. Write about an object you keep but rarely use.
5. Recall a memory that still surprises you.

At some point, every story begins.

Turn the page when you're ready.

Notes:

Part Two

The Core Prompt Collection

Notes:

The Core Prompt Collection

Stories rarely announce themselves. They arrive quietly — in a glance, a hesitation, a door opening, a thought that refuses to leave. This section is the heart of the collection: a series of prompt clusters designed to invite those moments forward.

Each cluster explores a particular narrative force. Some focus on movement. Some on tension. Some on stillness. Within each, you will find a short thematic introduction, core prompts to spark beginnings, optional deep-dive expansions to explore further, and a weekly challenge for when you wish to stretch your practice.

There is no expectation that every prompt be completed. Instead, notice which ones draw your attention. Curiosity is often the first sign of a story taking shape.

Open where you feel called.

Begin without urgency.

Let the story reveal itself in its own time.

Notes:

CLUSTER ONE

The Unexpected Beginning

Every short story begins with a threshold moment — the instant when ordinary life shifts and something else steps forward. It may be quiet or abrupt, gentle or unsettling. What matters is that something changes, and the character steps across without yet knowing what waits ahead.

The prompts in this cluster explore beginnings already in progress: conversations mid-stream, journeys underway, discoveries unfolding. Trust the movement. Allow the opening to carry you forward before you concern yourself with destination.

Core Prompts

1. A character opens a door they were certain was locked.
2. The first sentence of the story begins in the middle of an argument.
3. Someone receives a message that was never meant for them.
4. A routine journey is interrupted by an unexpected companion.
5. A character realises they are being watched — but not by whom.
6. A phone rings after midnight. No one speaks on the other end.

7. A character finds an object they lost years ago.
8. A conversation begins with the words, "I need to tell you something."
9. A character steps into a room they have never seen before — in their own house.
10. A stranger uses the protagonist's name without introduction.
11. A character wakes in a place they do not recognise.
12. A celebration is cut short by sudden news.
13. A photograph appears that no one remembers taking.
14. A simple favour leads to an unexpected obligation.
15. A letter arrives with no return address.

Deep Dives

Some ideas ask to be explored more slowly. Here are some gentle ways to extend a prompt - optional paths for when you feel curious, ready to linger, or eager to see what else a single beginning might reveal.

Use them when a story feels alive enough to follow further. Skip them when it does not. Both choices are part of the practice.

1. Write the opening scene without explanation. Let context emerge only through action and dialogue.
2. Rewrite the same opening from another character's perspective. Observe what shifts.
3. Place the beginning in a distinctly Australian

setting — a suburban cul-de-sac, a country highway, a beach car park at dawn, a train platform in winter — and allow the environment to shape tone.

The Weekly Challenge

Write a complete short story that begins with a disruption, however small. Let that single shift guide every choice that follows. When you finish, return to the opening paragraph and ensure it contains the seed of everything that comes after.

Notes:

CLUSTER TWO

A Moment That Changes Everything

Not all turning points arrive with drama. Often, they appear as small, almost ordinary moments — a sentence spoken, a glance held too long, a choice made in haste, a silence left unbroken. Only later does the character understand that something essential shifted in that instant.

The prompts in this cluster explore those subtle pivots. They invite you to write the scene where a story quietly changes direction — where one moment divides what came before from what must now follow.

Do not rush toward resolution. Stay inside the moment. Let its weight reveal itself.

Core Prompts

1. A character agrees to something they don't fully understand.
2. A truth slips out unintentionally.
3. Someone says, "I'm not coming back."
4. A character witnesses something they were never meant to see.
5. A door closes — and does not reopen.
6. A familiar place suddenly feels unfamiliar.
7. A character deletes a message before sending it — then regrets it.

8. Someone offers help that cannot be refused.
9. A character realises they have been misremembering an important event.
10. A casual comment lands with unexpected force.
11. A character chooses to stay when leaving would be easier.
12. A long-held belief quietly dissolves.
13. A character hears their name spoken in a context they did not expect.
14. A promise is made under pressure.
15. A character understands something too late.

Deep Dives

Some ideas ask to be explored more slowly. Here are some gentle ways to extend a prompt - optional paths for when you feel curious, ready to linger, or eager to see what else a single beginning might reveal.

Use them when a story feels alive enough to follow further. Skip them when it does not. Both choices are part of the practice.

1. Write the turning-point moment in real time, slowing the scene to capture physical sensation, breath, sound, and small movements.
2. Remove all dialogue from the scene. Convey the shift through action alone.
3. Write the same moment twice: once as the character experiences it, and once as they remember it years later.

The Weekly Challenge

Write a story in which nothing visibly dramatic occurs — yet by the final paragraph, the reader understands that everything has changed. Trust subtlety. Let implication carry the weight.

Notes:

CLUSTER THREE

Secrets and Revelations

Every story holds something back. A piece of information withheld. A feeling unspoken. A history left in shadow. Secrets create tension not through what is shown, but through what is hidden — and revelations reshape a story the moment they surface.

The prompts in this cluster explore concealment and disclosure. They invite you to write the space between what is known and what is not, and the moment when that space collapses.

Let the truth arrive in its own way — gently, suddenly, or painfully. Trust the character's reaction to guide the scene.

Core Prompts

A character discovers a letter never meant to be found.

Someone admits to a lie they have carried for years.

1. A photograph reveals a presence that should not be there.
2. A child repeats something they were not meant to hear.
3. A character learns they have been living under an assumption that isn't true.
4. A long-kept secret is revealed in public.
5. A character overhears a conversation that changes their understanding of someone they

love.

6. A hidden object is uncovered during an ordinary task.
7. A character is confronted with proof they cannot deny.
8. A stranger knows something deeply personal about the protagonist.
9. A confession arrives too late to repair the damage.
10. A character realises they have misunderstood their own past.
11. Someone breaks a promise of silence.
12. A revelation is delivered casually, without awareness of its impact.
13. A truth emerges in the middle of an unrelated conversation.

Deep Dives

Some ideas ask to be explored more slowly. Here are some gentle ways to extend a prompt - optional paths for when you feel curious, ready to linger, or eager to see what else a single beginning might reveal.

Use them when a story feels alive enough to follow further. Skip them when it does not. Both choices are part of the practice.

1. Write the revelation scene twice — first showing the discovery, then showing the immediate aftermath. Notice how the emotional tone shifts.
2. Place the revelation in a mundane setting —

a kitchen, a supermarket aisle, a suburban driveway — and let the ordinariness heighten the impact.

3. Write the moment of revelation without naming the secret directly. Let the reader infer it through reaction.

The Weekly Challenge

Write a story where the central secret is never explicitly stated, yet the reader understands exactly what has been revealed by the final paragraph.

Notes:

CLUSTER FOUR

The Stranger

A stranger is a disruption by nature. They arrive carrying unknown history, unseen motives, and the quiet power to change the emotional balance of a room. Sometimes they stay. Sometimes they vanish. Either way, their presence leaves a trace.

The prompts in this cluster explore encounters with the unfamiliar — new arrivals, unexpected visitors, brief crossings of paths, and the tension that lives in not knowing who someone truly is.

Allow curiosity to lead. Let the stranger reveal themselves slowly.

Core Prompts

1. A stranger arrives at the door asking for someone who no longer lives there.
2. A character sits beside an unfamiliar person on a long journey.
3. Someone new starts work in a place where routines are well established.
4. A stranger seems to recognise the protagonist — but the protagonist has never seen them before.
5. A visitor stays longer than expected.
6. A stranger offers help without being asked.
7. A new neighbour moves in and refuses to answer personal questions.

8. A character meets someone who knows their hometown intimately.

9. A stranger leaves an object behind after a brief encounter.

10. Someone unknown joins a small gathering uninvited — yet no one asks them to leave.

11. A character realises they have been watched by a stranger for some time.

12. A stranger tells a story that feels uncomfortably familiar.

13. Someone new enters a group and immediately changes its dynamic.

14. A character receives advice from a stranger they cannot ignore.

15. A chance meeting repeats — again and again — until it no longer feels accidental.

Deep Dives

Some ideas ask to be explored more slowly. Here are some gentle ways to extend a prompt - optional paths for when you feel curious, ready to linger, or eager to see what else a single beginning might reveal.

Use them when a story feels alive enough to follow further. Skip them when it does not. Both choices are part of the practice.

1. Write the scene from the stranger's perspective instead of the protagonist's. What does the stranger notice first?

2. Write the encounter using only dialogue. Allow speech patterns to reveal character.

3. Place the meeting in a distinctly Australian setting — a country pub, a suburban train station, a coastal caravan park, a rural servo — and let place influence tone.

The Weekly Challenge

Write a story where the stranger never reveals their purpose for appearing — yet their presence alters the protagonist's life in a lasting way.

Notes:

CLUSTER FIVE

The Ordinary Made Strange

Some of the most memorable short stories begin with the familiar. A routine task. A well-known place. A gesture performed a thousand times before. Then, with the smallest shift in perception, the ordinary becomes unfamiliar — and the story begins to breathe.

The prompts in this cluster invite you to look again at what you think you already know. To notice the overlooked. To linger in the mundane until it reveals something unexpected.

Stay with the moment. Let observation do the work.

Core Prompts

1. A character notices a small detail in their home that has never stood out before.
2. A routine commute feels suddenly different — and the character can't explain why.
3. A familiar meal tastes unfamiliar.
4. A character hears a common phrase spoken in a way that changes its meaning.
5. A daily chore reveals something long forgotten.
6. A character watches a neighbour's routine and realises it has changed.
7. A familiar song plays in an unexpected place.

8. A character finds something in their pocket that they don't remember putting there.//
9. An everyday object breaks — and it matters more than expected.
10. A character sees their reflection and notices something new.
11. A routine phone call feels different this time.
12. A familiar street looks altered in a certain light.
13. A character overhears ordinary conversation that suddenly feels significant.
14. A well-known scent triggers an unanticipated memory.
15. A character performs a daily action and realises they are doing it for the last time.

Deep Dives

Some ideas ask to be explored more slowly. Here are some gentle ways to extend a prompt - optional paths for when you feel curious, ready to linger, or eager to see what else a single beginning might reveal.

Use them when a story feels alive enough to follow further. Skip them when it does not. Both choices are part of the practice.

1. Write the scene focusing only on sensory detail — sight, sound, texture, taste, smell — and allow the emotional shift to emerge naturally.
2. Write the moment twice: first as the character experiences it, then as an outside observer would describe it.
3. Set the scene in an unmistakably Australian

everyday environment — a suburban kitchen, a backyard clothesline, a corner shop, a beach walkway — and allow place to shape the realism.

The Weekly Challenge

Write a story in which nothing dramatic happens externally, yet by the final paragraph the reader understands that something internal has quietly changed forever.

Notes:

CLUSTER SIX

The Choice

Every story turns on a decision. Sometimes it is dramatic and visible. Sometimes it is silent, almost imperceptible — a thought accepted, a truth denied, a step taken in one direction rather than another. Choice is where character reveals itself most clearly. It is the point where desire, fear, history, and consequence meet.

The prompts in this cluster explore moments of decision — impulsive, reluctant, courageous, or quietly inevitable. Stay with the weight of the moment. Let the character feel the cost before they act.

Core Prompts

1. A character says yes when they meant to say no.
2. Someone chooses to leave without saying goodbye.
3. A character decides to tell the truth — after years of silence.
4. A door is open in front of them. They must decide whether to walk through.
5. A character chooses to forgive someone who does not ask for forgiveness.
6. Someone decides to stay in a place they have always planned to leave.
7. A character deletes evidence that could change

everything.

8. A choice must be made before time runs out.
9. A character decides to trust someone they barely know.
10. A long-held plan is abandoned in a single moment.
11. A character chooses themselves for the first time.
12. Someone decides not to intervene — and must live with the outcome.
13. A character chooses to remember something they have tried to forget.
14. A decision is made in silence, without announcement.
15. A character chooses the harder path.

Deep Dives

Some ideas ask to be explored more slowly. Here are some gentle ways to extend a prompt - optional paths for when you feel curious, ready to linger, or eager to see what else a single beginning might reveal.

Use them when a story feels alive enough to follow further. Skip them when it does not. Both choices are part of the practice.

1. Write the decision moment entirely from inside the character's thoughts. Let hesitation and justification unfold on the page.
2. Write the same moment with no internal monologue at all. Show the decision only through physical action.

3. Place the choice in a recognisably Australian setting — a long country road, a coastal headland, a backyard at dusk, a quiet suburban intersection — and let the landscape echo the internal turning point.

The Weekly Challenge

Write a story where the central choice happens in the middle of the narrative rather than at the end. Allow the remainder of the story to explore the consequences of that decision.

Notes:

CLUSTER SEVEN

The Disruption

Most lives are built on expectation — routines, assumptions, quiet agreements about how the day will unfold. Disruption arrives when those expectations fracture. Something goes wrong. Something interrupts. Something refuses to proceed as intended.

Disruption is not always loud. It can be a missed call, a delayed arrival, a sentence that changes the atmosphere of a room. Whatever its scale, it forces characters to adapt, resist, or break.

The prompts in this cluster explore moments when control slips away and the story must find a new direction.

Let the disruption stand. Do not fix it too quickly.

Core Prompts

1. A character arrives late to something that cannot be paused.
2. A carefully planned event is cancelled without explanation.
3. Someone unexpected appears at exactly the wrong moment.
4. A power outage changes the course of an evening.
5. A character loses something essential — wallet, keys, phone, or proof.

6. A long-anticipated conversation is interrupted.
7. Bad news arrives during a celebration.
8. A character's transport fails, leaving them stranded.
9. A message arrives that contradicts everything previously believed.
10. A character is prevented from doing what they intended.
11. Someone breaks a rule that was never meant to be broken.
12. A minor inconvenience escalates into something larger.
13. A character is forced to share space with someone they wish to avoid.
14. A planned ending is no longer possible.
15. A story begins one way — then must suddenly change course.

Deep Dives

Some ideas ask to be explored more slowly. Here are some gentle ways to extend a prompt - optional paths for when you feel curious, ready to linger, or eager to see what else a single beginning might reveal.

Use them when a story feels alive enough to follow further. Skip them when it does not. Both choices are part of the practice.

1. Write the disruption as a chain reaction. Show how one small problem creates another.
2. Write the disruption without describing the

cause. Let characters respond before the reader fully understands why.

3. Place the disruption in an everyday Australian setting — a school pickup zone, a weekend market, a suburban backyard gathering, a country train line — and allow familiar surroundings to heighten the sense of things going wrong.

The Weekly Challenge

Write a story where the disruption arrives late in the narrative. Allow the first half of the story to build calm expectation — then let the interruption reshape everything that follows.

Notes:

CLUSTER EIGHT
The Quiet Ending

Not all stories end with revelation or resolution. Some end with a door closing, a breath released, a thought left unfinished. A quiet ending trusts the reader to feel what remains unsaid. It lingers rather than declares. It echoes rather than explains.

The prompts in this cluster explore conclusions that do not announce themselves — endings shaped by acceptance, recognition, resignation, tenderness, or simply the passage of time.

Do not rush toward closure. Allow the final moment to settle naturally. Trust restraint.

Core Prompts

1. A character watches something disappear from view.
2. A conversation ends without the important thing being said.
3. Someone leaves a place they will never return to.
4. A character realises the moment has passed.
5. An object is put away carefully, as if for the last time.
6. A character stands in a familiar place, seeing it differently.
7. A promise is remembered rather than fulfilled.

8. Someone falls asleep knowing tomorrow will be different.
9. A character listens to a sound fading in the distance.
10. A door closes gently behind someone.
11. A character accepts something they cannot change.
12. A familiar routine continues, altered in a subtle way.
13. A character reads something once more, then sets it aside.
14. A final glance is exchanged — or avoided.
15. A story ends in the middle of an ordinary moment.

Deep Dives

Some ideas ask to be explored more slowly. Here are some gentle ways to extend a prompt - optional paths for when you feel curious, ready to linger, or eager to see what else a single beginning might reveal.

Use them when a story feels alive enough to follow further. Skip them when it does not. Both choices are part of the practice.

1. Write an ending where the character does not speak. Let gesture and observation carry the emotional tone.
2. Write the final scene without naming the emotion you wish to convey. Allow the reader to feel it indirectly.
3. Place the ending in a distinctly Australian

setting — a beach at dusk, a veranda chair, a country road stretching away, a suburban street under streetlights — and allow place to hold the closing mood.

The Weekly Challenge

Write a story that ends one sentence earlier than feels comfortable. Stop before explaining. Let the silence after the final line do the work.

Notes:

Part Three

Creative Boosters

Notes:

Creative Boosters

Not every writing session begins with a blank page and a single prompt. Some days you already have a scene forming, a character whispering, or a fragment of dialogue waiting to be explored. On those days, what you need is not a beginning — but a spark that tilts what already exists into motion.

The tools in this section are designed to do exactly that. They are small narrative catalysts: twists, fragments, voices, objects, openings. You can use them on their own, combine several together, or layer them onto any prompt from the earlier clusters.

There is no correct method. Simply choose what draws your attention and allow it to alter the direction of your thinking.

A slight shift is often all a story needs.

1. Twist Generators

Every story benefits from surprise — not always dramatic, but meaningful. A twist reframes what the reader believes they understand. It creates depth, tension, or emotional contrast.

Introduce one twist into a scene or story:

1. A character has been lying about something minor — until it becomes significant.
2. Someone arrives earlier than expected.
3. A character realises they are not where they thought they were.

4. A promised event does not happen.
5. An apology arrives from the wrong person.
6. A character discovers they have misunderstood a relationship.
7. Something believed lost is found — or something believed found is lost.
8. A character overhears their own name in an unexpected context.
9. A planned confession is interrupted.
10. A character chooses not to reveal what they know.
11. Allow the twist to change direction, not simply add drama.

2. Character Sparks

Characters often arrive as fragments — a gesture, a habit, a contradiction. These sparks offer starting points for people who feel alive on the page.

Choose a character spark from the list below. Build a moment around it. Let the character reveal themselves through action rather than explanation.

1. A person who avoids mirrors.
2. Someone who keeps every receipt they've ever been given.
3. A character who speaks rarely, but always with precision.
4. Someone who is generous with strangers and harsh with family.
5. A character who is afraid of being forgotten.

6. Someone who laughs at inappropriate moments.
7. A person who carries an object for luck, without believing in luck.
8. Someone who cannot say no.
9. A character who collects endings — of books, relationships, conversations.
10. Someone who never asks questions.

Choose one. Let them move through a moment. Watch who they become.

3. Setting Sparks

Place is never neutral. It shapes mood, pace, and behaviour. These settings offer a foundation for scenes to unfold.

1. A nearly empty train platform at dawn.
2. A backyard during a summer storm.
3. A coastal town in the off-season.
4. A fluorescent-lit supermarket late at night.
5. A country road with no reception.
6. A school car park after the last bell.
7. A hospital waiting room.
8. A pub just before closing.
9. A living room where no one sits in the same chair anymore.
10. A beach at low tide.

Choose a place. Listen to its atmosphere. Allow the setting to lead the scene.

4. Object Prompts

Objects carry memory, weight, and emotional residue. Place one at the centre of a scene.

1. A key with no known lock.
2. A cracked phone screen.
3. A ring removed and placed on a table.
4. A handwritten note folded many times.
5. A suitcase that has not been unpacked.
6. A photograph with someone cut out.
7. A jacket left behind.
8. A cup with lipstick on the rim.
9. A children's toy found in an adult space.
10. A watch that has stopped.

Allow the object to influence action and thought.

5. Dialogue Starters

Sometimes a story begins not with description, but with a voice already speaking.

Begin a scene with one of these lines:

1. "I wasn't supposed to tell you."
2. "We need to talk — now."
3. "You don't remember, do you?"
4. "I thought you'd never come back."
5. "This isn't what you think it is."
6. "I'm leaving in the morning."
7. "Promise me you won't ask why."

8. "It wasn't meant to happen like this."
9. "You owe me the truth."
10. "Don't say anything. Just listen."

Let the conversation reveal what the narrator will not explain.

6. First-Line Hooks

The first sentence sets a tone, a question, or a direction. These openings are invitations rather than instructions.

1. The day began like any other, until it didn't.
2. I knew something was wrong before anyone spoke.
3. The message arrived at 2:17 a.m.
4. We agreed never to discuss that night again.
5. By the time I understood what I'd done, it was too late.
6. Nothing in that house stayed where it belonged.
7. I have never told anyone what really happened.
8. The stranger knew my name.
9. We were all pretending.
10. I didn't expect to be the one who stayed.

Select an opening. Step inside its promise. Follow where it leads.

Notes:

Part Four

Advanced Writing Challenges

Notes:

Advanced Writing Challenges

Wherever you've opened this book, you've encountered beginnings, moments, revelations, choices, disruptions, and endings. You have gathered sparks, fragments, characters, and places.

The challenges in this section are designed to gather those elements and apply gentle pressure — not to force creativity, but to strengthen trust in your instincts.

Each challenge introduces a constraint: time, perspective, limitation, or structural play. Constraints are not obstacles. They are focusing tools. They quiet the inner editor and invite momentum.

Approach these exercises with curiosity rather than performance. The goal is not to produce perfect stories.

The goal is to practice finishing.

1. The 30-Minute Story Sprint

A short story does not always need long preparation. Sometimes speed allows honesty to surface before self-doubt intervenes.

Preparation (5 minutes)

- Choose one setting from the Setting Sparks.
- Choose one object from the Object Prompts.

- Choose one dialogue starter.
- Write them at the top of your page.

Writing (20 minutes)

Set a timer. Write a complete scene in which:

- Two characters share a moment of tension or connection.
- The chosen object appears naturally in the scene.
- The dialogue starter is spoken at a turning point.
- The scene ends with a subtle shift in understanding.

Do not pause to edit. Let the story move forward without correction.

Reflection (5 minutes)

Underline one sentence that feels alive.

Circle one moment you want to explore further later.

Stop there. Completion is the practice.

2. Writing Under Constraint

Limitation sharpens attention. When certain tools are removed, others grow stronger.

Choose one constraint and write a short story within it:

- No dialogue.
- No internal thoughts.
- Only one setting.

- Only five sentences.
- No use of the words said, thought, or felt.
- Begin and end with the same image.
- Tell the story in reverse order.

Let your chosen constraint guide structure rather than restrict imagination.

3. Perspective Shifts

Every story holds more than one truth. Changing perspective reveals hidden dimensions.

Choose one of the following:

- Rewrite a previous story from another character's point of view.
- Tell the story from an observer who does not understand what is happening.
- Tell the story from someone remembering the event years later.
- Tell the story from the point of view of an object present in the scene.

Notice what emerges when the narrative lens moves.

4. Genre-Bending Stories

Short fiction is an ideal space for experimentation. A shift in genre alters tone, rhythm, and expectation.

Choose a story you have already begun — or start a new one — and write it as:

- A quiet domestic drama.

- A mystery with an unanswered question.
- A speculative or surreal tale.
- A comedic misunderstanding.
- A minimalist literary vignette.

Allow genre to shape the story's atmosphere without forcing cliché.

5. The Story-in-a-Day Challenge

This challenge is simple: begin and finish a story in one day.

Morning — Choose a prompt. Write freely for twenty minutes.

Afternoon — Continue the story. Bring it to an ending.

Evening — Read once. Make only essential corrections. Then stop.

Do not polish. Do not perfect. Let the story exist as is.

Completion builds confidence.
Confidence builds consistency.

Part Five

Bonus Writer Tools

Notes:

Bonus Writer Tools

Writing is not only about inspiration. It is also about returning — to the page, to the practice, to the unfinished fragment that suddenly feels alive again. The tools in this final section are designed to support that return.

They are simple by intention. They require no preparation, no explanation, and no perfect conditions. Use them when you feel stuck, when you feel playful, when you feel uncertain, or when you simply want to write without making too many decisions first.

Consider these pages your quiet back pocket — always available, always ready.

1. Prompt Dice Tables:

Chance is a generous collaborator. When you allow randomness to choose elements for you, expectation loosens and curiosity steps forward.

If you have a six-sided die, roll once for each table. If not, use a random number generator from one to six. Combine your results and begin writing.

Table One — The Encounter

1. A meeting at a train platform
2. A chance crossing in a supermarket aisle
3. A shared wait in a hospital reception
4. A conversation at a bus stop

5. An encounter on a quiet beach
6. A meeting in a café just before closing

Table Two — The Tone

1. Awkward politeness
2. Quiet curiosity
3. Unspoken tension
4. Unexpected warmth
5. Subtle irritation
6. Immediate familiarity

Table Three — The Complication

1. A misunderstanding arises
2. Someone leaves abruptly
3. A truth slips out
4. A third party interrupts
5. Time runs out
6. Something is forgotten

Table Four — The Object

1. A set of keys
2. A folded note
3. A mobile phone
4. A jacket
5. A photograph
6. A cup of untouched tea

Combine your rolls. Write a scene of 500 to 1,000 words. Allow the elements to guide the story rather than control it.

Example Roll

Table One: 2 — A chance crossing in a supermarket

Table Two: 4 — Unexpected warmth

Table Three: 3 — A truth slips out

Table Four: 6 — A cup of untouched tea

Resulting Prompt: Two people cross paths in a supermarket. Their interaction begins with unexpected warmth. During the exchange, a truth slips out. A cup of untouched tea is involved.

Begin writing.

2. Random Prompt Picker

On days when decision-making feels heavier than writing, let selection be effortless.

Close your eyes. Open the book at random. Place your finger on the page. Use the prompt beneath it. If no prompt sits there, use the nearest one above or below.

There is no wrong choice. The page you open is simply the one you needed today.

3. Monthly Writing Tracker

Consistency is built gently, not forcefully. A writing habit does not require daily output. It requires return.

At the beginning of each month, note the days you intend to write. Mark each day you do — even if only for five minutes. At the end of the month, look at what you accomplished rather than what you missed.

Momentum grows quietly. If you wish, the Monthly Writing Tracker on the next page provides a space to notice your rhythm over time.

Now you have reached the end of this section, this book closes — but your practice does not.

You now have beginnings, turning points, revelations, choices, disruptions, endings, sparks, challenges, and tools. All that remains is the return.

Open anywhere.

Begin again.

Open Anywhere

Monthly Writing Tracker

Monthly Writing Tracker

A writing practice grows through return, not force. This tracker is not a measure of productivity, but of presence. Mark each day you sit with the page — whether for five minutes or an hour. At the end of the month, notice what you did rather than what you missed. Small consistencies quietly build strong habits.

Month: _____

My intention for this month:

_____

_____

_____

_____

_____

Writing Days (Tick each day you write, even little bits.)

☐ 1   ☐ 2   ☐ 3   ☐ 4   ☐ 5   ☐ 6   ☐ 7
☐ 8   ☐ 9   ☐ 10 ☐ 11 ☐ 12 ☐ 13 ☐ 14
☐ 15 ☐ 16 ☐ 17 ☐ 18 ☐ 19 ☐ 20 ☐ 21
☐ 22 ☐ 23 ☐ 24 ☐ 25 ☐ 26 ☐ 27 ☐ 28
☐ 29 ☐ 30 ☐ 31

What I worked on

_____
_____
_____
_____

One thing I discovered this month

_____
_____
_____

A line I liked

_____
_____
_____

Next month, I want to explore

_____
_____
_____

Notes:

Notes:

Open Anywhere

Note Pages

Use the following pages to collect:
- Lines you like
- Character sketches
- Scene fragments
- Possible titles
- Observations from daily life

Return to these pages when a prompt calls for something new. Your own notes will become your richest resource.

.

About the *Open Anywhere* Series

Writing rarely begins with a perfect plan. More often, it begins with a spark — a half-formed idea, a sudden image, a sentence that arrives out of nowhere. The *Open Anywhere* series was created to honour that moment.

Each book in this collection is designed to meet you exactly where you are in your writing journey. No pressure. No prerequisites. No expectation that you call yourself a "real writer" before you begin. Just an invitation to open a page and let something new unfold.

Every volume follows the same trusted structure — prompt clusters, creative boosters, and writing challenges — so once you feel at home in one book, the others become familiar companions. The genres change. The sparks shift. But the rhythm stays the same: *choose, imagine, write.*

Some readers use these books for daily practice. Some dip in when they feel stuck. Some bring them to writing groups, classrooms, libraries, or quiet corners of cafés. However you use yours, know this: *the goal is not perfection. It's momentum.* It's experiencing the simple joy of putting words on a page.

The *Open Anywhere* series is part of a wider creative ecosystem built for writers — a belief that stories grow best in good company. Wherever you are on your writing path, you're welcome here.

So keep this book close. Return often. Let it surprise you.

And when you're ready for a new genre, a new challenge, or a new direction — there's another volume waiting.

Open anywhere. Your next story is already inside.

Where the Series Goes Next

The *Open Anywhere* series has been designed as a collection of companion books — each exploring different genres.

Future books are already taking shape behind the scenes. Others will emerge as writers like you reveal what they need next. When they arrive, they will be written in the same familiar format — ready to open at any page, ready to begin again.

Stay in Good Writing Company

These books are created through *Scribbly*, the writing community initiave from *BookTree Publishing*. If you'd like to hear when new books in the series are released — along with free resources, mentoring opportunities, and writing projects — you are warmly invited to visit us at www.scribbly.com.au

Our Invitation

Keep this book close. Return when the page feels quiet. Trust that every visit matters, and when the next volume appears, you will already know how to begin.

Open anywhere.

Your next story is already inside.

About the Author

Katy More is a writer, mentor, and creative guide with a deep commitment to helping writers find their way to the page — and stay there with confidence. She is the founder and creative heart of *Scribbly,com.au*, a quiet, supportive space for writers built on care, clarity, and community, and she brings practical experience from years of mentoring, editing, and writing across genres.

Katy also contributes her design and communications expertise to **BookTree Publishing,** where she helps authors navigate the journey from idea to finished book with calm purpose and clear guidance.

Across her work — in books, publications, blogs, workshops, and conversations — Katy has long championed the idea that storytelling need not be intimidating. She believes that short stories, in particular, offer writers a generous and immediate way into craft, voice, and creative momentum. Her approach blends thoughtful structure with room for discovery, encouraging writers to trust their instincts and return to the page without self-judgement.

Katy lives and works in Queensland, Australia, where she assists both emerging and experienced authors, leads community writing projects, and continues to develop resources that help writers feel seen, heard, and capable. She writes in her own name as well as through the diverse voices of the *Scribbly* collection, always bringing practical experience, curiosity, and support to every project.

About the Publisher

BookTree Publishing is an Australian independent publisher dedicated to helping writers bring meaningful books into the world — professionally, ethically, and with care.

Based in Queensland, *BookTree* works alongside authors at every stage of the publishing journey. Their focus is simple: practical pathways, transparent guidance, and publishing solutions that respect both the writer and the reader.

BookTree believes that publishing shouldn't feel mysterious or inaccessible. It should feel like a partnership — where ideas are nurtured, books are built well, and writers are supported to make informed choices about their creative futures.

Produced by *Scribbly*.com.au

Scribbly.com.au is the creative community and mentoring division of *BookTree Publishing* — a home for writers who want encouragement, resources, and good company along the way — all run by volunteers.

Through free mentoring, writing resources, workshops, podcasts, and community projects, *Scribbly* pairs experienced writing mentors with intelligent creative tools to support writers — from first tentative ideas to finished manuscripts and beyond. It is a place where curiosity is welcomed, questions are encouraged, and no writer is expected to walk alone.

The *Open Anywhere* series is an initiave of *Scribbly* — supported by *BookTree*— shaped by years of working directly with writers, listening to where they get stuck, what inspires them, and what helps them return to the page. These books are a natural extension of that mission: simple, friendly tools designed to help writers begin — again and again.

To learn more about ***BookTree Publishing***,
visit: www.booktreepublishing.com.au

To explore *Scribbly*'s free writing resources,
visit: www.scribbly.com.au

Because stories grow best
in good company.

www.ingramcontent.com/pod-product-compliance
Lightning Source LLC
LaVergne TN
LVHW051219070526
838200LV00064B/4970